THE
CODE

Jeff Gottesfeld

SADDLEBACK
EDUCATIONAL PUBLISHING

red rhino
b**OO**k s™

With more titles on the way …

SADDLEBACK
EDUCATIONAL PUBLISHING
www.sdlback.com

Copyright ©2014 by Saddleback Educational Publishing

ISBN-13: 978-1-62250-894-5
ISBN-10: 1-62250-894-7
eBook: 978-1-63078-026-5

Printed in Guangzhou, China
NOR/0714/CA21401177

18 17 16 15 14   1 2 3 4 5

Chris

Age: 13

Proudest Moment: got all As on his last report card

Looking Forward to: a trip to Alaska

Favorite Food: peach cobbler

Best Quality: stands up for others

PHIL

Age: 13

Biggest Problem: being bullied by his older stepbrother

Wants to Become: a race car driver

Favorite Food: beef jerky

Best Quality: knows he could be nicer

1
THE CODE

It was a school fight like all the others. A big kid picked on a small kid. The small kid got his butt kicked. Other kids made a ring to watch and cheer.

Truce?

The big kid was Phil Hartz. Phil was strong. The small kid was Sam Colton. Sam was a wimp. Phil liked to pick on wimps.

Phil used to pick on Chris Marks. That was why Chris did not try to stop the fight. He just stood there and watched. Just like all the kids in his seventh grade class. There were yells and shouts. It was not a fair fight. Phil did what he wanted. Sam fell to the ground. Phil kicked him in the ribs just for fun.

That was when Mr. Jones ran onto the field. He was the principal. He hated fights. He said all kids could get along. Chris was not so sure. By the time Mr. Jones got there, the fight was over.

"Who started this?" Mr. Jones was mad.

Phil shrugged. "It just happened."

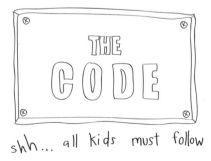

THE
CODE

shh... all kids must follow

That was a lie. Chris knew it. No one said a word. The kids had a Code. No one ever talked. Chris did not like the Code. He did not like it one bit. But he did not want to be picked on by Phil. No one did. It was too bad that Sam got beat up. But Chris did not think it could be stopped.

"Come on, kids. Someone saw. Talk. Please." Mr. Jones looked from kid to kid. Then he called the names of the best students. "Mary Lopez. Alan Parker. Chris

Marks. Sylvie Pollock. Tai Browne. Come with me!"

Chris gasped. Mr. Jones wanted to talk to him? He wanted to know how the fight began.

They all went to Mr. Jones's office. The principal closed the door.

"It's safe," he told the kids.

No one said a word. If any of them told, all the kids would know someone broke the Code. This is why Chris did not talk.

"Oh, come on," Mr. Jones said. "You guys can stop this. All you have to do is say who started the fight. Phil, right? Don't want to say it? Write it down. I'll leave the room. Just write the name on a file card."

I can't write it down. That still breaks
THE
CODE

Mr. Jones found file cards. He put them on his desk. He found pens too. Then he left.

The kids were alone.

Tai shook her head. "I'm out."

"Me too," Alan said. "You know why."

"Me too," Mary agreed.

Chris felt Sylvie's eyes on him. He turned to her. She put one finger to her lips. He knew what she wanted to say. *The Code.* Break it and a kid could get hurt.

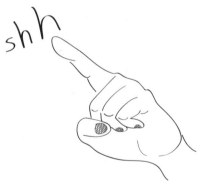

When Mr. Jones came back, he looked at the file cards. They were blank. He got mad.

"You kids! You know Phil started it. I need your help to show it."

Chris looked down at his feet. He felt his face get red. But he did not say a word.

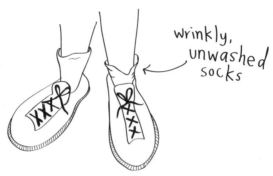

wrinkly, unwashed socks

Mr. Jones shook his head. Then he pointed to the door. "Get to class. Go."

Chris went. Phil was right there in the hall. So was Phil's friend Rodrigo. He could tell no one talked to Mr. Jones. He grinned. Chris hated the grin on Phil's face. He hated it so much.

2
CHEATER!

Chris went back to class. All the kids were still buzzing about the fight. Sam was there. Sam's face lit up when Chris looked at him. The little guy came over to talk. "What did you say to Jones?"

Chris shook his head. "Not a thing."

"Didn't Jones ask who started it?"

"Sure. But I didn't say. It isn't that I didn't want to. But … you know."

Sam nodded sadly. "Yeah. I know."

"That's it. If I were you, I would stay out of Phil's way. He belongs in a zoo."

A huge voice boomed out behind Chris. "I

heard that!"

Chris turned. There was Phil. His chest was all puffed out. He had an evil look on his face. Chris's lunch turned over four times in his belly. Ugh. Now he was on Phil's *I'm-gonna-mess-you-up* list for sure. Why could he not keep his mouth shut?

"Relax, dude," Phil told him. "Call me what you want. Just keep your mouth shut."

The teacher, Ms. Santos, came in. "Pop quiz! Map of America. You are so lucky."

The whole class moaned. Ms. Santos was

big on pop quizzes. Then she could tell if the kids did their homework. Chris knew the whole map, no sweat. His family did car trips every June. He had been to forty-five of the fifty states. He even knew the big cities. When Ms. Santos gave out the quiz, Chris did the whole thing in less than a minute. There were no goofs. He looked over at Sylvie. She had it down cold too.

I've always wanted to visit here

Then he looked at Phil. Phil sat three seats to the left in the same row. Phil was staring to his own left.

My seat

Phil's seat

Chris figured he was looking out the window. But no. Phil was staring at his bud Rodrigo. Rodrigo was doing the quiz. But he was also touching his cheek with his right hand. One finger. Two fingers. Three fingers. Then one finger a—

Oh no.

It was like lights snapping on in Chris's mind. Rodrigo and Phil. They were cheats!

Chris checked out Ms. Santos. Was she watching? Nope. She was on her iPad. She didn't see a thing. When she did look up,

Phil and Rodrigo cooled it.

Ms. Santos was online shopping

"Okay! Time's up. Pass your quizzes to me," Ms. Santos told the class.

All the kids passed their quizzes to the front of the room. Ms. Santos took them. Sometimes she would grade them right away. Sometimes she took them home. Either way, she had no idea that two kids cheated. Chris knew, though. And it made him feel as bad as the fight had. Maybe worse. He wanted to tell. But he couldn't.

The Code. *The Code.*

3
DARE TO DATE

Chris pulled back on the string. The bow got taut. The arrow was ready. He let it fly.

The arrow whizzed to the target at the other end of Sylvie's yard. *Smack*! The hard tip ripped into it.

"Seven!" Sylvie shouted when she saw where the arrow hit. "Good job."

"Not as good as you," Chris said.

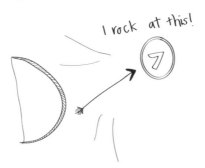
I rock at this!

"We'll see."

Sylvie got her own bow. She was such a small girl. Chris did not know how she could even pull back the string.

"And ..."

She let fly. Bull's-eye.

"You're the best at this," Chris told her.

"I've been doing it more. You're still a newbie."

Chris made a face. "Did you ever want to be like Robin Hood? I mean, to shoot an apple off Phil Hartz's head? I'd like to see him sweat."

"It was William Tell, not Robin Hood.

And I'm not the girl to do it." Sylvie put down her bow.

"He cheated on the quiz today."

Sylvie shrugged. "Kids cheat all the time. It's not your prob. It's the school's prob."

"And he beat up Sam." Chris was mad all over again.

Sylvie looked at him. "Chris, get a grip. You can't change it. Let it go." She smiled. "Speech is done. Want a Froze-Froot?"

"Froze-Froot"

Chris grinned. Sylvie always made him feel better. They knew each other since they were babies. Their dads shared a boat. They went to the same church. He liked Sylvie. Really *liked* her. But if they got to be a couple, they might not ever be friends after they broke up. And they would break up. Everyone broke up.

Sylvie had a big old house. Chris lived in a new one, with all new stuff. He liked Sylvie's more. It had brick walls and a wood floor. It had—he was not sure of the right word—a soul.

Sylvie's house has "SOUL"

"I'll take a peach—"

"You want to go to the movies next week?"

Chris stopped dead. He was about to ask for a peach Froze-Froot. But Sylvie had asked him a thing way bigger.

"Did you just …"

Sylvie smiled. "We're on school break next week. We can't fish. What else will we do?"

"Play guitar?" Chris was good for his age. He loved old rock. One day he wanted to be in a band. Sylvie played a little. But she liked sports more.

"The movies would be more fun. So?"

"So, what?"

Sylvie held up her hands. "Chris. Don't you get it? I just asked you out. You can say yes. Or you can say no. I vote yes."

Chris hit his own head with his palm. He

was so dense. He had wanted this for so long. Only he wanted to be the one to ask.

Oh well. There was only one thing to do.

"Yes."

Sylvie smiled. "Smart guy. Let's get the Froze-Froots."

Will you go out with me?

☐ NO   ☑ YES

4
THE VISITOR

"Chris!"

Chris was in the bathroom with his guitar. The bathroom had the best sound in the house. He opened the door to answer his mom. "Yeah, Mom?"

Best room in the house BY FAR

"Someone at the door for you!"

Huh. Who could it be? Sylvie for sure. She was the only one who just came over. But his mom never stopped her at the door. Had to be someone else.

Still with his guitar, Chris padded to the door. His mom was with a kid his age. Chris's jaw fell open. The kid was Phil Hartz.

"Hey, dude," Phil said. "Nice ax. Didn't know you played."

Chris's mother smiled. "Well. I'll just go back inside. Have fun. Chris, your friend can stay for dinner, if you'd like."

Friend? Friend?! Chris wanted to yell at his mom. Phil was not his friend. Phil was bad news.

"Okay, Mom," was all he said.

"Your mom is nice," Phil offered.

Chris looked at him. "Why are you here?"

Phil pointed his chin toward the front of

the house. "There's a bench out there. Let's sit."

Chris left his guitar by the door. He followed Phil to the bench. "So?"

Phil made a *V* with two fingers. "Hey. I come in peace. I owe you a big thanks."

"No you don't."

"I do. You saw what went down with Sam and me. You kept it shut. You saw me getting a little help on the quiz. You kept it shut. I know the other kids. They won't talk. But you? Man, you're a lone wolf. Except for that Sylvie girl. Good to know you know the drill."

Phil clapped Chris on the back with his open palm. Chris felt ill. He had been ready to let the whole thing go. Forget what happened with Sam. Forget about the test. Now Phil would not let him forget.

"Okay." Chris stood. "I gotta go back in and play more."

Phil stood too. "Chris. Don't you get it? When my friends do good for me, I do good for them. Laser tag next week. You in?"

Friends? Chris could not believe what Phil was saying. He couldn't talk.

"What? You don't want to be friends with

me? Really? You don't want to be my friend? We can do it that way." Phil got a hard look in his eyes. "Easy as pie."

Chris thought of Sam that day. On the ground. Kicked. Hurt. No. Chris did not want to be a not-friend of Phil's. Besides. Maybe he could help to change Phil.

"I'm in," he decided aloud. "As long as Sylvie is too."

"Word," Phil said.

Phil's fist came toward him. Not for a punch. For a fist bump. The deal was sealed.

5
"SAY SORRY"

"Chris! Watch out!"

Chris spun. To his left was a guy with a laser gun. To his right was a wall. Before the guy shot at him, Chris dove. He got to the wall before he could be hit. Good thing too. One more hit and he would be out of the game.

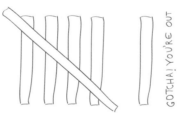

GOTCHA! YOU'RE OUT

"Chris, you rock!"

He turned to his right. Phil. Phil gave

him a big wave. "You are a laser tag stud!"

Chris grinned. He felt great. He was here with a bunch of kids. All were friends of Phil's. Sylvie was there too. They had played two games so far. Chris was on the winning side both times. When they chose teams for game three, Chris was the first guy picked.

Chris crawled to his left. He had a clear shot at Rodrigo. He lifted his laser tag gun. He fired. Yes! Rodrigo was out of the game. With Rodrigo gone, Chris's team won fast.

Rodrigo

All the kids came to high-five Chris. Even the kids who had lost. Chris was pumped.

For the first time ever, he had a rep. All that target shooting with Sylvie had helped.

The lights went on. The time for playing was over. The kids went to the snack bar.

Chris found Sylvie. "Having fun?" she asked.

"The best," Chris said.

"See? Phil isn't so bad."

Chris nodded. It was true. Phil was not so bad. But he would be better if he did not beat up kids. Or cheat.

Sylvie seemed to read his mind. "You thinking about Sam?"

"Yup. Phil needs to say sorry."

"No way. He won't do that."

"I know." Chris got a juice and drank it. His throat felt dry. Could he really tell Phil to say sorry? Sylvie was right. Phil might not like that.

"So, what are you going to do?"

Chris frowned. It was fun to be Phil's bud. But he wanted to feel good about himself too. For that, Phil had to say, "Sorry."

He saw Phil alone by the door. This was his chance.

"Excuse me," he said to Sylvie.

"Where are you going?"

"I'm going to do what I have to do."

He went to Phil. Phil fist-bumped him. "Hey, Mr. Laser Tag. You're only ever on my team. Don't say no."

"Okay." Chris just stood there.

"What?" Phil asked. "Is that all you can say?' "

Chris shook his head. "No, I have more."

"Then say it, dude," Phil urged.

Chris bit his lip. This was the time. Like it or not. He could speak up. Or he could forget it.

"Fine," Chris said to Phil. "I think you need to say sorry to Sam."

Am I really

going to say this?

6
DORKY HERO

Phil's eyes got wide.

"You want me to do *what*?!"

Phil's Mean Look

Chris knew Phil heard him fine. He still said it again. "Say sorry to Sam. In school. When we get back. For hitting him. Kicking him. Like that."

Chris gulped. He had just called out Phil Hartz. He didn't know what Phil would do.

But Chris had to live with himself. That meant Phil had to say sorry.

"Or what?" Phil asked. He had a mean look in his eyes.

"Or … well …" Chris stopped talking. Did he have the guts to say what had to be said? "Or you're a jerk."

Phil rubbed his chin with his hand. He pushed back his thick hair. "Oh?"

Chris felt weak. Phil hated him now. He was sure of it.

"Sorry," Chris muttered.

"Mm-kay," Phil said. "Okay. Monday. I'm all over it. Heck. He can even come to laser tag next time. As long as he's on your team."

Chris wanted to shout. Or high-five all the other kids. His plan had worked! He had stuck his neck out. Phil could have cut it off. But Phil had done the right thing. It was like Chris helped Phil be a better person.

"That's ... that's great! So ... see you in school next week."

He almost danced back to Sylvie.

"What are you so up about?"

"You gotta hear this!" He pulled Sylvie close and told her the news.

"Wow. Look at you, Chris. You're a hero."

Chris shook his head. "No, I'm not."

"To me you are." Sylvie grinned at him and took his arm. "When Sam hears this? You'll be a hero to him too."

The first day back at school, Chris hung with Sam. That was when Phil was going to say sorry. Chris wanted to be there.

They saw Phil come outside.

"I'm scared, Chris," Sam said.

"Don't be," Chris told him. "Phil is cool."

"My side still hurts from when he kicked me."

Phil came close. It was just like last time. Kids formed a ring. If Phil wanted to hit Sam, he could. It was what the kids wanted.

"Fight! Fight! Fight!" The chant went up.

"Let's get out of here." Sam's voice was as high as a girl's.

It was too late. Phil was right there. He put his hand out for a shake. Sam took it. Then Phil turned to the ring of kids. "You all hear me? Show is over. I'm done. Hurt

Sam and you hurt me. Get it?"

The kids got it. Everyone left. Then Sylvie ran up to Chris. "Now do you think you are a hero?"

"All I want to be is a hero to you," he said. The words were out before he saw they were so dorky.

"Cheese fest!" Sylvie shouted. "Come on, dorky hero. Walk me to class."

7
CHURCH SURPRISE

The next Sunday, Chris went to church with his mom and dad. Sylvie was there too. After the service, there was a line outside the door. The pastor, Pastor John, waited there to shake hands and say hello. Chris liked him. He was a real guy.

Pastor John →

He's a Real Guy!

Chris shook the pastor's hand. "Hi, Pastor John."

The pastor smiled. "Chris Marks. Just the boy I wanted to see."

Chris gulped. "Did I talk too much today? Did I mess up?"

"Ha! Mess up? You did great this week. I know about Phil Hartz and that Sam boy."

"But how?" Phil did not go to this church. Neither did Sam.

The pastor smiled. "Good news moves fast." He pointed to the sky. "I bet *he* knows too. Good for you. Keep it up."

Sylvie was on the lawn. Chris went over to see her. "What did Pastor John want?"

"He said I did good with Phil. And that God knows."

Sylvie laughed. "I don't know about God, but every kid knows. They think you rule. If you told them all to jump? They'd just ask, 'How high?' "

Chris had no idea if that was the case. He did not want to be the kid who ruled. He just wanted to be normal. A kid who went to the movies with a girl like Sylvie. It would be his first real date. But he felt ready now.

"Hey," he said to her. "I thought we were going to the movies."

"We did laser tag."

He shook his head. "Laser tag with Phil is not the movies with you."

Sylvie's eyes shined like bright stars.

"Are you asking me to the movies?"

"Did you do all your homework?"

"I sure did," Sylvie said. "You?"

"Yup." Chris nodded. "So. How about five o'clock? My mom told me she would drive."

"What?" Sylvie gave a yelp. "You asked your mom?"

"Hey. A guy has to be ready at all times."

He winked at Sylvie, then walked off to meet his mom and dad. He didn't get far before he heard his name called. "Yo, Chris!"

Whoa. Chris stopped. He knew the voice, but it was not a voice he had ever heard at church. Could it really be …

He turned. Yes. It was Phil Hartz. Why

was *he* here?

Phil walked over to him. "You didn't expect me, huh? Well, I knew you would be here. And I didn't want to show up at your house again. Got a sec? We need to talk."

8
FIRST DATE

The movie was over. It was just the kind that Chris liked. A lot of stuff blew up. The bad guy was super evil. And the good guy had to be smart to save the world. He was there with Sylvie. She had on a green dress and sandals. She looked fab. And she held his hand the whole time.

sylvie looked FAB!

He knew he should have been on top of the world. But he didn't feel that way. He felt down after his talk with Phil at church. Really down. Sylvie could tell too.

"Okay, time's up," she told him as they went into the lobby.

"Time's up for what?"

"For you to *not* be Mr. Dark Dude. There is something on your mind. So, spill it."

Chris made a face. "You can tell?"

Sylvie nodded. "Yup. I know you better than you know you." She grinned so all her teeth showed. "See? I don't bite. So, tell me. Even if it's that you never want to go out with me again. I can take it."

There was a bench in the lobby. Above it was a movie poster. It was of the movie they'd just seen. Chris knew his mom was in the car outside. But it was fine for her

44

to wait a little. Sylvie was right. Something was on his mind. No. Some*one* was on his mind. If he could not tell Sylvie, who could he tell?

They sat. He turned to her. "Sorry. I've been a jerk."

She took his hand. "No. You're thinking about something. What?"

"Not what. Who."

"More please?"

Chris sighed. "After I church, I got a surprise."

NOT A good surprise

"Some other girl asked you out? Give me her name. I'll mess her up." Sylvie laughed to show she didn't mean it.

"No girl. A guy. Phil Hartz."

Sylvie's eyes got huge. "Phil Hartz asked you out? Did you say yes?"

Upset as he was, Chris laughed. "Funny. But no. He didn't ask me out. He said Rodrigo is sick. He asked me to 'help' him if there's a pop quiz from Santos."

He felt warm breath on his arm as Sylvie pushed it from her lungs. "Wow. *Help*, meaning *cheat*."

"Exactly."

"What are you going to do?"

"We have to go." Chris didn't want to make his mom wait too long. It was nice of her to drive them. He said nothing more.

He had been thinking about what to do all during the movie. He still had no answers. He thought he had changed Phil. He thought Phil was his friend. But Phil was the same guy he was before. Only he didn't beat up kids. Chris wondered if that would change if he said no. Maybe he would get beat up. And what about the Code? Even if he said no, he couldn't tell anyone.

He stepped toward the doors, then out into the fresh air. He heard the beep as his mom tapped the car horn.

"Any great ideas?" he asked Sylvie.

She shook her head. "Nope."

"That makes two of us."

They got into the car and didn't say a word all the way home.

9
CAREFUL WHAT YOU WISH FOR

It was a great day to be outside. Sunny. Warm. No wind. There were games of freeze tag and dodge ball everywhere. But Chris wasn't playing. Instead, he got the other good students in Santos's class to meet him near the main school doors.

Meeting spot

Sylvie was there. Mary Lopez. Alan Parker. Tai Browne. And Sam too. He had just finished talking to them when he saw Phil head for the basketball court.

"Okay, wish me luck," he said.

"Good luck, man!" Alan said.

"We're with you," Sylvie added.

Chris started toward Phil. "Hey, Phil!"

Phil saw him. A slow, easy grin spread over his face. "Chris, dude, good to see ya. You think about what we talked about at the church?"

This was it. The moment of truth. "Phil, I did. And I have to say, what you want me to do? It's just wrong."

Phil looked hurt. "You're my bud, right? And you won't help me out?"

Chris shook his head. "Because it's wrong. Look. Let's say you cheat. And get a high grade. Other kids will get pushed down because of that. That's not fair. And if a lot of kids cheated, well, that would mess up kids who play by the rules. You see?"

For one moment, it seemed like Phil did see. Then his face turned dark.

"Are you saying you won't help me?"

Even though he had a plan, Chris got scared. "No. I'm not saying that."

Phil relaxed. "Good. Cause Rodrigo is out sick. I need you. You know the code for the right letters to mark? Put your fingers on your ears for the question number.

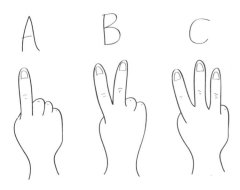

The Cheat Code

Put them on your cheek for the right letters. One finger is *A*. Two is *B*. Like that. Got it?"

Chris nodded. "Got it."

"Good," said Phil. "And keep your mouth shut. See you in class."

Well, Chris thought. *Phil wants to cheat? He needs to be careful what he wishes for.*

10
BREAK
THE CODE

Ms. Santos gave out the quiz. "This one is easy. Everyone can get them all."

Chris looked at it. She was right. It was easy. In fact, it was the same quiz she had given before school break. The same questions about the same map. Chris figured Phil would not even have to cheat. He turned to look at Phil. Phil opened his hands, as if to say, "Get with it! I don't have all day."

"Fine," Chris said in a whisper no one could hear. "You want help? You get help."

He signaled the answers to Phil, one after the next. *A*, *B*, *C*, *D*. And then, *D*, *C*, *B*, *A*. And finally, *A* and *B* again.

Phil gave him a thumbs-up when the quiz was done. Ms. Santos took the quizzes. She told the class to read. She was going to grade them right then. It only took about five minutes. When she was done, she called out names.

"Chris? Tai? Sam? Alan? Sylvie? Phil? See me in the hall. *Now*."

Instead of making fun or laughing, the rest of the class was dead quiet. It was as still as a church. Chris led the others outside.

"What's going on?" Phil asked him.

Chris shrugged. "Beats me."

"If I'm busted?" Phil asked. "You will be too."

Ms. Santos got them to stop talking. "I'll be blunt. You kids all have the same answers on this quiz. But you five?" She pointed to Chris, Sam, Tai, Alan, and Sylvie. "You got perfect scores on this quiz last time. This time? Fail! And I want to know why." Then she pointed to Phil. "And you? You cheated off one of these students. Which one?"

Chris spoke up before Phil cou   ld. "He cheated off me," Chris said. "But we five made a pact before. We hate that he cheats. And that we're not supposed to say anything. Well, we're talking now. We got the same bad grades on purpose. So we could prove to you we are in this as a group."

"You're a rat," Phil growled to Chris. "You'll pay."

Chris The Rat?!

"Try it," Chris said boldly.

Ms. Santos thought for a moment, then

sent everyone inside but Chris.

When she knew they were alone, she spoke. "You have a lot of guts," she told him. "And it was smart, doing it with the others. But you all get Fs. Everyone flunks, you know." She frowned.

Chris made a face. "Hey. It's just one quiz. We'll make it up."

"I'll be watching Phil like a CIA drone now," Ms. Santos promised. "Go back inside."

CIA Drone

Chris went inside. He saw the hate on Phil's face. He saw the fist. He knew he had to be ready after school. Phil might come after him. But after class, he didn't see Phil for the rest of the school day. No one had seen Phil. Chris felt a little better. Maybe Ms. Santos had reported him to Mr. Jones. When the bell rang, he and Sylvie left school together.

"That was great what you did today," she told him.

"It was—oh no. Look!"

Across the school yard, Phil was running to them. To his left was Rodrigo, the kid too sick to be in school that day. He looked fine now.

"Chris!" Phil shouted. "I'm going to mess you up. And then, I'm going to mess up—"

Another fight?

"Nothing," Chris tried to stay calm. "You will mess up nothing. And no one."

"Says who?" Phil growled.

Chris took a deep breath. "Says me. And my friends."

It was almost like magic.

Chris had talked to the other kids in class about what might happen after school. They were so happy for what Chris and his friends had done that they agreed to help. They formed a ring around Chris, Sylvie, Phil, and Rodrigo. Then they linked arms.

That's when Sam stepped into the ring. "No more fights. And no more cheating. We will turn you in. We'll turn anyone in! We're with Chris and Sylvie. Now. Forever!"

For a long time, Phil and Rodrigo did not move. Then they walked toward the ring of kids. It opened to let them out. And then it closed in on Chris and Sylvie. There were shouts of joy and a ton of high fives. The Code had finally been broken.

Forever Broken